C. J. Ballingall Birrell

Two Queens

a drama

C. J. Ballingall Birrell

Two Queens
a drama

ISBN/EAN: 9783337303273

Printed in Europe, USA, Canada, Australia, Japan

Cover: Foto ©Andreas Hilbeck / pixelio.de

More available books at **www.hansebooks.com**

TWO QUEENS

A DRAMA

BY

C. J. BALLINGALL BIRRELL

GLASGOW

JAMES MACLEHOSE & SONS

Publishers to the University

1889

TWO QUEENS

DRAMATIS PERSONÆ.

Edward the Sixth.

Lord Northumberland, - - Father-in-law to Lady Jane.

Lord Suffolk, - - - - Father of Lady Jane.

Lord Howard, - - - - Friend of Queen Mary.

Various Lords and Councillors.

Lord Guildford Dudley, - - Husband of Lady Jane.

Father Feckenham, - - - Queen Mary's Confessor.

Scheyfne, Renard, - - - Austrian Ambassadors.

Queen Mary.

Lady Ann Wharton, - - - Her Lady of honour.

Lady Jane Grey.

Lady Suffolk, - - - - Lady Jane's Mother.

Lady Northumberland, - - Lady Jane's Mother-in-law.

Angela, - - - - - Lady Jane's Waiting-Woman.

Mistress Underhill, - - Wife of one of the Tower Atten-
dants.

TWO QUEENS.

ACT I.

SCENE I.—HUNSDON HOUSE.

Princess Mary and Lady Ann Wharton.

Princess. My Lady Ann, you have been with me
    long,
When came you first to Court?
    Lady Ann.   Madam, I scarce can tell,
The count of years runs far into the past.
    Princess. Then I'll be minister to your remem-
    brance.
You came to me before my mother died :
You soothed my tearless anguish and despair
By the large sympathy of honest eyes

When words were fatal,—tenderness, a crime.
She was an Empress' daughter, Lady Ann,
Queen of all England, yet she died alone,
Refused in death the sight of her own child,
Poor soul! I weep to think on't.

> *Lady Ann.* Ah, madam, there is sorrow every-
> where.

> *Princess.* But not like ours, like ours it cannot be.

For you, you others need not hide your grief,
Quench the hot streams that well from wounded
  honour,
And scarf quick sores with agonizing splendour:
You can cry out and beat upon your breast,
But I must see my mother die alone,
Nor ever by the quiver of an eyelid
Betray the rebellious torture of control.

> *Lady Ann.* Secret suffering is a cruel thing.

> *Princess.* It makes the heart grow hard : the
> tender sapling

Warps into knots, and the unsightly bark
Cancels the promise of a noble tree.
'Twas so they twisted me, thwarted and maimed me
Upon the rack of time : I have borne much,   .

Suffering has left me little more to learn.

Lady Ann. But it is past, the future is your own.

Princess. The future, Lady Ann, I have no future ;
The old wound's quick, and starts at such a word.

Lady Ann. Madam, you have some grief I do
not know.

Princess. It is all grief, blackness and foul despair.

Lady Ann. Oh, madam ! do not, do not speak
such words.

Princess. I must, or thought will choke me : you
know well
I have not wasted words through all these years.
When have I ever murmured or complained ?
But now the final struggle is at hand,
I warn you now, the ultimate throw with fate.

Lady Ann. Oh, if it be not too much pain to
speak,
Tell me the present trouble.

Princess. My Lord Northumberland makes plots
to slay me,
Even the Emperor bids me leave the land.

Lady Ann. How terrible the abyss of secret crime !
And will you leave?

Princess. Not while the breath is in my body, no!
'Tis only cowards abdicate their right.

Enter Attendant.

Att. My Lord Northumberland waits.

Princess. How can he dare to come? Oh! it is
    cruel!
Go to him, Lady Ann, keep him in talk
Until my constancy be recomposed.

                  [Exit Lady Ann.

Princess. What is the malignant mystery of my
    nature
That calls for such stern judgment? What the flaw
In my soul's health that needs such bitter medicine?
Was it my parent's guilt or mine that writ
My destiny in such characters of woe?
Be calm, my heart, blot out all show of sense,
He comes, and I must see him.

Re-enter Lady Ann with Lord Northumberland.

Princess. I lack the words to bid you welcome,
    sir,
In sudden apprehension of your coming,
No trivial errand summons you so far,
Speak, I entreat you, I await your words.

Lord North. I have received your missive—

Princess.   What ! no more.

Lord North. Madam, it is enough :

The King, your brother, lies at point of death.

Your absence here fetters our certain action,

There being thousand forms and ceremonies

To which you must conform upon succession.

The errand, this, which brings me in such haste—

To bid you back with me to London.

    Princess. The King is worse?

    Lord North.   Grievously, madam :

That certain foe whom none can ever foil

Stations his outposts at the city gates ;

Now, point by point, the vital ramparts yield

And soon the citadel of life must fall.

    Princess. 'Tis a sore case, my Lord Northumber-
        land.

Yet in my narrow range, I have made note

How closely youth may run its race with death.

Youth is the surest physic of all ill.

Nay, every Spring we hear the King must die.

    Lord North. It is no saying now.

    Princess.   Nor then I'll warrant,

Until the time was past. I do not question
The stubborn claim of matters ceremonial,
But this perpetual oracle of woe
Has razed the present danger. I am fixed.
While the King lives, I will not budge a foot.
 Lord North. Then, madam, I am bold, but you
  do wrong.
Pardon me, therefore, I must speak my mind.
How can a man o'ercharged with state affairs
Brood o'er a sick-bed with a woman's kindness.
I am a citizen in life's rough school,
And fitter to deal blows than bind the wounded,
Whence should I learn to match the asking eye
With its swift answer and fulfil requirement.
Your part it is, and should you fail therein
All men will blame you for indifference.
I speak in your own interest, who more fit
Than sister to attend a dying brother?
 Princess. My lord, your words are true, nay,
  gospel true :
And I most loath to set their weight aside,
Nor shall I blame the bluntness of your speech
As might most women,—but 'tis thus with me,—

Scarce in this country quiet can I live
Fenced from all ill by sedulous observance,
Nor have I secret springs of hidden strength
To nurse the King with life blood from my veins.
Lady Northumberland must fill my lack,
And I commend to her most loving care
The charge of my young brother. She can more
Than I in watchful tendance. That is all.
Bespeak the King for me my tender love,
And inmost grieving for his dolorous ailment.
Good morrow, sir, farewell.

> [*Exit Lord Northumberland.*

Princess. How my heart aches for that unhappy
    boy !
Poor child, I loved you not: my father's fault,
Who ate the grapes that set our teeth on edge.

> *Enter Lady Ann Wharton.*

Lady Ann. Madam, the Austrian Ambassador is
    here,
Urgent to see you. What ! is aught amiss ?

Princess. Saw you my lord protector as he went ?
Or did he see the other ?

Lady Ann.   Madam, I think not,

The Ambassador came by the private gate
Beneath this chamber.

Princess.   Then it is well so far,
Let none know of his coming, least 'of all
The one you wot of, my worst enemy.
It is not open violence I dread,—
The stealthy prick of an assassin's dagger,
The secret malice of corroding poison,
Might rid me quickly of my strongest friend.

  Lady Ann. Madam, the surety of an Emperor's
    name
Clothes him in stronger panoply than steel.

  Princess. 'Tis slippery walking on earth's mountain
    tops,
There's mist there,—yes, and precipices, too,
And ice to freeze the bones. I know it well.
The good Ambassador waits,—I'll see him then.
But yet be wary, not a step so light
But it may wake an adder. Have a care.

Re-enter Lady Ann with the Austrian Ambassador.

  Princess. He whom we know is here to-day :
    perchance,
Is not yet gone.

Scheyfne. Can he have dared such boldness?

Princess.   Know it well.

Therefore I almost fear to see you now.

Scheyfne. Why?

Princess.   Hush! there's a step!

A door's beyond that curtain. Softly, there,

The stair is winding.

Enter Lord Northumberland.

Lord North. Madam, before I leave, I speak

  once more;

Are you prepared I publish your resolve,

Reveal to men the love you bear the king,

It will make honour for you?

Princess.   Sir, once more,—-

Publish my words to every wind of heaven,

Show up to all the monster of sour humour,

The harsh step-sister gloating o'er his ill,

Enlarge indignant speeches of persuasion,

Men will believe your words.

Lord North.   This jesting is ill timed,

Whose interest but your own can be at stake.

Princess. Sir, leave my interests in their proper

  charge.

Lord North. Some one was with you now?

Princess.   My interest still.

Lord North. You should be careful, stories may

  arise

Which may prove harmful. Trust my experience.

Princess. I trust in no man born. Is that enough?

Pardon me, sir; indeed, I am not well,

I pray you, leave me.

    .   [*Exit Lord Northumberland.*

Princess. Softly, come forth, the enemy has gone.

            Enter Scheyfne.

Sir, tell me all you know, the very worst:

Anything better than uncertainty.

What is he doing now?

Scheyfne. While the King lives your life at least

  is safe.

Princess. So much I thought, else he had seized

  me now;

Yet why should one who meditates such crime

Pause for the mere breath of a dying boy?

Scheyfne. Northumberland is wise: he knows

  right well

Ten thousand loyal swords leap from the scabbard

To guard your Highness from intended ill.
Therefore he waits till cunning pretext work
To bring you craftily within his toils.
The lord protector masks his real purpose
To pose as saint till time convict him sinner.

    Princess. O villain! worse than villain, seeming
        saint!
Such words he spoke; had you not warned me first,
I would be riding to determined death.
This life is hateful. What of the young King?
You know what credit I can give his tale.

    Scheyfne. Sinking, fast sinking, like a stranded hull
Washed by each billow nearer to decay;
'Tis possible a month he may survive—
No longer.

    Princess. Alas! alas! that I should grudge his time.
And yet it is so long to wait like this
When every moment's misery. Tell me more.

    Scheyfne. My lord protector tries a double game,
To play off France against the Emperor.

    Princess. France! 'tis a danger that would touch
        me home!
How does France view him?

Scheyfne. The French King trusts him as the Em-
    peror,
Well knowing that his word is light as sand,
Puffed to whichever side self-interest blows.
But still it is a danger, I must warn you,
The Emperor holds it so.
    Princess.   Hide nothing from me,
I see some villainous tidings are in store,
I know it well.
    Scheyfne.   Madam, I am recalled.
    Princess. You speak my doom, sir, uttering words
    like these.
    Scheyfne. Another comes more skilled in ways of
    men,
Fit to match Frenchmen on their proper ground,
Well liked of all, and one that knows right well
To tune his accent to a lady's ear.
    Princess.   To me blunt truth
Is dearer far than smooth indifference.
He has not been my stay through all these years.
It is not yet too late, you cannot go.
    Scheyfne. Madam, my summons is beyond recall.
    Princess. I have given o'er my confidence in man;

My trust is in the God who judges right,
And loves to give the battle to the weak!

Scheyfne. Your Highness' cause stands not alone
with me,
Three-fourths of England's noblest youth send word,
Their sword defends you in the hour of peril.

Princess. Thanks for all such, but I have no one
near,
Like you, to brave Northumberland's displeasure;
The craven Lords of Council work his will,
Hoping for me the best, but doing nothing.

Scheyfne. I can do many things through alien
birth,
Impossible to them; they're yours in heart,
Despite the apparent show, believe me, madam.

Princess. I'll not mistrust your words, but men
are feeble,
And foes are strong, and each man serves himself.
'Tis natural so. But tell me one thing more
Of that poor victim, luckless Lady Jane.

Scheyfne. 'Tis said she had no mind to wed his
son;
Her heart was with young Hertford.

Princess.   So I heard.

We both are in his toils, and she is young

And fair and ignorant, while I am old

And skilled in ways of men.   I pity her.

To win or lose, we both must suffer pain.

But who will help me, sir, when you are gone?

I have no friends to guide my faltering steps.

 Scheyfne.   While the King lives, you have no
  cause for fear,

And ere the last breath leaves your royal brother,

Horsemen will ride to bear the tidings here.

Then pause not, stay not, fly for very life,

Until you reach the Howards' seat in Norfolk;

They will protect you in the time of need.

Be calm meanwhile, yet with a careful ease,

As inly mourning the young King's decline.

But I must leave you, madam, or be missed.

 Princess.   Farewell, farewell, my best and truest
  friend,

The one sincerely honest I have known.

For most men are obedient to the whim;

Ready at times to do a random kindness,

Or, as unthinking, do a random ill.

And I must trust to their uncertain humour,—
Is it a marvel that my heart should fail?
Did not my mother die before her time,
Heart-broken in her widowed solitude,
Murdered—oh, not by blows that take the sense—
But deeper wounds that lacerate the soul.
Did I not know her when in royal state
Courted by troops of reverential suitors?
Did not I see them leave her in distress
And flock as gladly to her rival's side?—
Such memories are ill omen of success
And poison life with bitter recollection.
The whole herd tramples on the fallen steer,
As they will now, my augury is plain.
And yet I thank you for your watchful care,
You shall be ever in my heart, adieu.

   Scheyfne. Ah, madam, I shall live to see you queen.
   Princess. I hope, indeed, but with a heavy heart.
                                 [*Exit Scheyfne.*

Alone! the power is all upon his side!
Yet am I triply armed with right divine;
The crown of England rests upon this brow
If heaven restore it to its rightful heir.

B

My mother, for thy sake I must be queen !—
To purge the stain from thy untarnished honour,
That sunk thy drooping spirit to the grave.
Be armed, my heart, the day of trial comes,
Leave woman's fear to those less nobly born,—
A royal spirit knows no touch of fear.

SCENE II.—GARDEN IN FRONT OF LORD SUFFOLK'S HOUSE.

*

Maidens Singing.

Hail, glorious sun ! that dost the kindling vine
  Flush with the radiance of celestial fire !
To thee we lift our hearts, propitious shine
  On budding hope, with bloom of young desire.

See how each flower spreads out her shining breast,
  Delighted thy caresses to receive !
Watch how the fields grow white at thy behest,
  Whose golden braids the tangled sunbeams weave.

Hail, glorious sun! that dost the kindling vine
    Flush with the radiance of celestial fire!
To thee we lift our hearts, propitious shine
    On budding hope, with fruit of young desire.

            Enter Lady Jane.

  Lady Jane. Pray you no songs, for I am sad at
    heart.

Last night in dream methought I saw the King,
Clad all in white and crowned with kingly state,
Stretching his hands to reach me through the gloom,
With pleading eyes that mutely made request :—
" Come to me, cousin, I am all alone,"
And when I woke I knew it was a dream,
But still his presence fills my waking thought,
Wherefore my heart keeps vigil far away
And summer brightness is but mockery.

  Maid. Is the King dying, madam?

  Lady Jane.   Ah! who knows
Why do you speak such harsh unfeeling words?
The King is suffering, suffering far away,—
My most dear kinsman, at the point of death.

  Second Maid. Madam, there's one comes running
    in hot haste

Who wears the livery of Northumberland.

Lady Jane. Bid him approach that I may hear his
      words,
What message, man, brings you in such hot haste?
Not sorrow, tell me, quick !

Mess. Nay, but a humble harbinger, your grace,
To advertise my mistress' near approach,
Who comes with Lady Sydney and Lord Dudley,
Your honoured husband : all are close at hand.

Lady Jane. Haste, maidens, lead this messenger
      within,
Bid him acquaint my mother, I wait here.
Like snow on summer's day are sudden meetings,
And aching bosoms presage naught but ill.

    Enter Lady Northumberland and Party.

Lady North. Good-morrow, sweetheart, from a
      loving friend,
The country air revives you, you look well,
Not pale as is your wont from musty books.
Come, Guildford there will frame a pretty speech
Where do the roses go when summer dies ?
We can tell that to-day.

Lady Jane.   Madam, he cannot tell ;

He has no knack of tongue, wanting in practice.
But still I keep you standing, you are tired,
Will you within?

    Lady North. Not a step further, pray you. Let us
      sit, ·
Are there not seats around yon spreading oak?

          Enter Lady Suffolk.
Good-morrow, madam, we take vantage of you:
I've seen you twice since you saw me in London.

    Lady Suff. May love increase for oftener acquaint-
      ance,
Bring the oak settle out and sit it here,
That seat's too low for all save youthful limbs.

    Lady Jane. What is the latest tidings of the
      King?
The thought of him scarce ever leaves my mind,
But certain news comes rarely.

    Lady North. Still very sickly; but we hope the
      best.
A woman doctor late hath done him good
With soothing herbs. His is a sickly youth,
Yet many a one that seemed to be as frail
Has reached a green old age, my husband says.

Lady Suff. Ah, no; the mind's too vehement for
  the strength,
And frets the feeble barriers of the soul.
His face had death's stamp when I saw him last
At our two weddings. Jane, do you remember
How our dear kinsman looked on you and smiled,
As though he watched you from another world.
I trembled at his sight.

 Lady Jane.   Ah, he is good!
And yet meseems o'erburdened with sad thought;
A youthful Atlas holding up the world,
Which crushes him to death.

 Lady North.   It is most true.
His mind is active far beyond his years,
Already planning princely charity.
The maintenance of the poor hath all his thought,
And he of late hath much discoursed thereon.
But to my errand. I am bid to fetch you
On urgent business to the Court to-morrow.
My husband waits your presence.—Lady Suffolk,
I see, is loath to lose you, but 'tis needful,
And tearful parting urges sweet return.

 Lady Jane. What is to do? Mother, can you be left?

Lady Suff. Nay, Jane, I pray you, tarry with me
here.

Lady North. Why ! 'Tis impossible, she comes
with me.

Lady Suff. Who has more right than mother to
her child ?

Lady North. 'Tis palpable to all in Nature's
teaching,
A woman shall be subject to her lord.

Lady Suff. I say Jane shall not leave me with
my will !

Lady North. Then without will perforce she needs
must leave.
Come, Lady Suffolk, do not make delay,
Jane will be well and come to you anon.

Lady Suff. I fear me, madam, if she go with you
She never, never, will return again.
They wish to make you, Jane, the Queen of England.

Lady Jane. But that I can be never: cease to
urge,
Lady Northumberland, and let me stay.

Lady North. Nay, my sweet daughter, but it may
not be.

My husband urgently demands your presence,
And I, myself, am come to fetch you hence.

Lady Jane. Then, dearest mother——

Lady Suff.   No, you shall not go.
I thought you had more firmness than be swayed
Against your will, but that you hate your mother,
Else you would wait with me and let them go.

Lady North. Nay, Jane, hear me, I am compelled
   to bring you :
The King himself it is desires to see you.

Lady Suff. Ay, ay, no doubt; to make a fool of
   you.
So, you will part a mother from her child?

Lady North. So, you will part a husband from
   his wife?
Be reasonable, madam, let her go,
Considering what the issue.   And you, Dudley,
Why stand you silent; have you naught to say?

Lady Suff. You tear her from my arms; I have
   no right,
No portion in the daughter whom I bore?

Lord Guildford. Jane, as my wife, I bid you
   come with me.

Lady Jane. How am I torn by these contending
   claims?
Mother, dear mother, 'tis my husband's claim;
Why do you make it hard for me to go?
   Lady Suff. Then take your choice: you see the
   last of me.
Bid your dear husband haste to get to horse.
I'll have no more of this. I wish you joy.   [*Exit.*
   Lady North. How dreadful is a passion uncon-
   trolled
In an old woman! Jane, show us the way.
The less delay the better suits my purpose.
                                    [*Exeunt.*
         Re-enter Lady Suffolk.
   Lady Suff. Gone! gone for ever, and beyond re-
   call!
How I have played into that woman's hands.
An endless sorrow is the care of children:
For all the love we lavish on their childhood
Is flung into the sea without return.
But yet I know Jane will not leave me thus,
She will not go from me without a word
For all my hardness.

Enter Lady Jane.

Lady Jane.   Mother !

Lady Suff. Ah Jane, my Jane, you have returned
    to me ;
You will not leave me, you have told them so.

Lady Jane. If marriage be a bond, how can that
    be ?

Lady Suff. Yours is no bond ; it was your father's
    doing,
Not mine, Jane ; I had never seen you wed
With my consent to upstart Dudley's son.
Renounce the marriage and stay with me here.

Lady Jane. You know not what you say, my
    dearest mother,
What is once done can never be made void.

Lady Suff. Therefore it is I would not have you
    leave me.

Lady Jane. Ah, mother dearest, you feel but for
    me
As every mother parting from her child,
Whose clear eyes see her in a shifting world
Bereft of guidance ; oh, I know your thought.
But whether good or ill attend their steps,

Mother and daughter at some time must part.
Wherefore, dear mother, do not hinder me,
But kiss me and embrace me ere I go.

    Lady Suff. Ah, Jane! I fear, I fear I know not
      what,
But something in this marriage makes me fear.
Mark my words, child, and trust your lady mother
No farther than you see her: but you're simple,
Learned in books, but not in ways of men,
Who take advantage of your innocence.
I deemed you once too simple—did not love you;
But time takes vengeance—scarce we meet in soul
When parting rends the too late-loving hearts.
Heaven's smile goes with you, daughter, where you
      go.
May you live long and happy and be blest!
But my heart fears.

                        [Exeunt.

Act II.

Scene I.—Sion House.

The King and Northumberland.

Ed. VI. When did you bid the judges come, my
    lord?
I wonder if my strength will bear me through
This parleying. Why should they thwart me thus?
Will they not even let me die in peace?
Woe to this country if my sister reigns?
You know her well—her stubborn resistance,
And steadfast cleaving to idolatry.
And in this land there is but that one left
To whom I safely can entrust the state,
My cousin most beloved, the Lady Jane.
    Lord North. Indeed, all men discourse her pass-
    ing wisdom,
A marvellous constancy in one so young;

Yea, with all gifts she is so meek of soul,
She wears her learning lightly as a flower.

Ed. VI. Wit, wisdom, beauty, modesty itself,
Can never countervail the weight of truth,
And steadfast perseverance in the right,
The precious dower of a sovereign soul.

North. Alas! the lawyers will not have it so.
Their purblind vision gropes in noonday night,
Not seeing aught beyond its narrow range,
Nor how the loss of one may profit many.

Ed. VI. They will see right, they will see truth
    to-day.
'Tis said men dying have a clearer view
Of past and future than at other times.
I, a king dying, will speak words of weight
That they must listen to the cause of truth.
Are they not yet come? Bring them if they
    are.

Enter Chief-Justice Montague, Sir Thomas Bromley,
    Sir John Baker, Marquis of Winchester, and
    others.

    Ed VI. Goodmorrow, sirs, bring you the letters
      patent?

I crave your pardon for a hasty greeting,
But business urges.

    Montague. Alas, your grace, we serve a stubborn
        master,
One that will bend before no private will;
Wherefore, though private will would do you service,
The sovereign will of right o'errules that plea.

    Ed. VI. What right, save Heaven's, can overrule
        my right
To instant execution of my will?

    Mont. Even angels bend obedient unto law,
Since order controverted breeds disaster,
No matter who the opposer; kingly power
Shows kingliest in its lawful exercise.

    Ed. VI. You put me off with quibbles—what is
        law?
What in the law forbids the letters patent?

    North. (*aside*) You kill the king by over-arguing.
Be niggardly of words—he cannot bear't,
Unless you'll have him drop before your eyes.

    Mont. Your father, sire, for eight and thirty years
Governed this realm in dignity and honour,
And, ere his death, seeing your tender youth,

Knowing the chances of uncertain life,
Bequeathed the crown, devising it to you
And to your sisters in direct succession,
Seeking thereby the welfare of the land
And so empowered by Act of Parliament.
Sire, what the nation's universal will
Hath so accorded, hath no private scope,
And nowise lightly may be set aside.
What by the writ of Parliament is fixed
Only by parliament may be annulled.
Wherefore in this, we cannot do your will
Touching the matter of the letters patent
To set in power your cousin, Lady Jane.

   Lord North. (*aside*) You'll slay him ere you go,
     his colour wanes.

   Ed. VI. It seems that parliament hath ampler
     scope
Than in my father's time?

   Mont.   Since most ancestral times,
So has it been, nor is it altered now.

   Ed. VI. Intolerable words, you goad my wrath!
Ye do but take advantage of my youth,
Forms of the law are your divinity,

For forms ye murder me : but I am set.

Forms I dispense with, write the letters patent.

    Mont. In study of your royal father's will

We find ourselves convict of treasonous blame

If we obey you.

    Ed. VI.   Treason to him or me,

What matters it? my servants are at hand

To cast my rebel subjects in the tower,

And ye are rebels, not obeying me.

But this I see—men love the rising sun

More than the setting, I am on the wane.

My sister hath suborned you to her will.

O miserable emptiness of show !

The common love that gilds men's dying hours

To me is wanting—I was born a king.

Ye do not know my sister nor the fate

From which I would save England—do not know,

Grey headed, full of honours, what it is

To die unheeded in unpractised youth.

The Gordian knot of life for me is cut,

And may not be unravelled,—I am the grave

Of all the good I purposed for my people;

And now ye throne another to annul

All I have done or would do for the land.

Oh! by the last breath of a dying king,

By all that sweetens life for other men,

I charge you that in this ye do my will.

Let men but see, let them in this behold,

My last anxiety was for my people.

 Mont. Sire, is there haply some small chamber
  where

We may confer apart, ere we would yield

To you our thought touching this weighty matter

Ed. VI. Speak to them for me, good Northumberland. [*Exeunt Lord Northumberland and*
     Judges—some wait behind.

 Suffolk. The King! the King! Fetch the physicians, haste!

 North. Is he gone, think you? Suffolk, chafe his
  hands.

How thin they are, like glass. What is ado?

 Howard. Look how the nail is broken! They are
  slow,

Physicians never ought to leave his side—

Here's a woman at last. Who is she, Suffolk?

 Suffolk. The king's physician and his only nurse.

       C

North. That looks not well for a Protector's care.

Woman. Rouse up, sir, see the noble lords attend,
'Tis but a swoon, my lords, you see he stirs.

    Ed. VI. Cassandra ! Cassandra ! They will not
      hearken to thy prophecy !

Suffolk. What is he thinking of ? these are strange
    words.

    Ed. VI. Gentlemen, do I wake or do I dream ?
Have I been long thus ? 'tis my tedious wont.
I have seen horrid sights, the fires of Spain
Burning in England, kindled by my hands.

    Suffolk. A dream, your grace, the judges are at
    hand
Ready to do your bidding.

    Ed. VI.   It is well.
I can die happy now, bid them approach ;
But spare their words, seeing my strength is small.

    Mont. Sire, we will do your royal highness' will,—
So be in writing you will make it known
That by command we altered the succession,
By you defended from the blame of treason.

    Ed. VI. Write what you will. I'll sign it with
      my hand,

And, with all haste prepare the letters patent,
Seeing our time is brief. No words but love,
The state in your hands and do good.—Farewell.

SCENE II.—SION HOUSE.

Lady Jane and Waiting-Woman, Angela.

Lady Jane. How strange that no one has awaited
    us !
Angela. It is an evil augury for the King.
Indeed, the house is very strangely hushed—
No one seems stirring.
Lady Jane.   'Twas good of him,
The King, I mean, to bid me here to see him.
We played as children not so long ago;
But he goes home so soon, too soon for us.
I was so near his age, just like a sister,
And like a sister now I mourn for him.
Poor King ! the crown has crushed his life.

Angela.   Dear lady, you are pale,

Your limbs are trembling.   Shall I fetch you wine?

Lady Jane. No, Angela, it is but passing faint-
  ness ;

It is the waiting and suspense undoes me,

I shall be well anon.   Ah ! Angela,

I never have seen death,—I tremble now,

My accents seem too gross for one near heaven.

Enter Northumberland, Northampton, Arundel,

Pembroke, Suffolk.

North. Heaven in its grace has called the King
  to rest,

His was an easy passing of the soul.

The King is dead, and you are Queen of England.

Lady Jane. Oh, sirs, what words are these? it
  cannot be

The King is dead—our noble, royal master !

North. The King, I say, is dead, and you are
  Queen.

Lady Jane. Gentlemen, sirs, this cannot be the
  truth ;

You have confused my sense with sudden tidings.

The King is dead, I scarce believe it yet,—

But more than this strange other—I am Queen.

But why should mighty nobles so conspire

To mock an ignorant girl?

    North. In very truth you are the Queen of Eng-
        land.

Look and behold the charter of that title

Signed by a thousand honourable names.

    Lady Jane. The dear, dear King is dead! Help,
        Angela!

    North.   The lady swoons.

I'll fetch my wife to help her. Here they come.

Enter Lady Northumberland and Lady Northampton.

    Lady Northumberland. Poor soul, o'ercome!
        Gentlemen, further back.

Bring forward the great chair and set her on't.

You were too sudden with unlooked for tidings.

But she revives, her eyes begin to tremble.

    Lady Jane. They said that I was Queen? How
        can that be?

    Lord North. The bill is here, and you will read
        it soon,

Signed by the best and noblest names in Eng-
    land.

Lady Jane. I thought the Lady Mary had been
        Queen;   .
Why is she set aside?

Lord North.   'Tis writ herein;
The Lady Mary is a stubborn Papist,
And by King Henry's will was set aside,
As was her sister.

Lady Jane.   Was't not o'erruled?
'Tis monstrous this—and yet the Lady Mary.—
My lord, these matters are too high for me,
Let it be on your truth that ye deal truly.

Lord North. The good King Edward hath before
        his death
Bequeathed the crown, devising it to you
And your descendants in direct succession.
So in his name we swear to honour you,
And if need be defend you with our lives.

                [*Reads the letters patent.*

Lady Jane. Then it is true.   There's comfort in
        the thought;
I see I reign not for myself alone,
But for the Church, to follow the king's aim,
A precious heritage bequeathed to me.

And in myself I know that I am weak,

But yet, though weak, I do desire the right,

And Heaven itself will guide my stumbling steps

To clearer knowledge.   Gentlemen, arise,

I am too faint for further conference,

But I shall see you soon.   Farewell.

> [*Exeunt Lady Jane, Lady Northumberland,*
> *Lady Northampton.*

Lord North. What think you, gentlemen, of your
  young Queen?

Pembroke. She's but a white rose, Dudley.

North. Rose royal, spite the colour of it, Pembroke.

You will all meet me at the Tower to-morrow

To welcome the young Queen?

> [*Exeunt all but Pembroke and Arundel.*

Arundel. What think you of this latest move of
  Dudley?

Pembroke. Not so loud, pray you; walls, they say,
  have ears,

And long ones in this place.

Arundel.   And asses too;

I speak no treason.   He's a clever man.

His head's as safe to come off with the one
As with the other: He does well to try.
  Pembroke. What think you of the Lady Mary's
    cause?
I heard the ambassador implored her grace
To leave the country ere the young King died.
  Arundel. It was a foolish thing to call back
    Scheyfne,
A quiet man who knew the country well.
Have you seen Renard?
  Pembroke.   Supped with him last night.
The Emperor's cause won't suffer, I'll be bound,
Whoever reigns.   'Tis we that have to suffer,
Who waver sadly in uncertain ways.
The eastern counties will.be all in arms
Before a week is gone.   There are my horses.
If Lady Mary get alive to Norfolk
I'll give my lord the slip; the citizens hate him
More than he reckons.   Will you come with me?

Scene III.—Keninghall Dining Hall.

Lady Howard and Daughter.

Lady Howard. I wish your father, child, were safely
    back !

Daughter. You're anxious-minded, mother, grown
    of late.
What is't you fear?

Lady How.   It is a shifting world,
And men must sometimes tremble.

Daughter.   Tell me, mother,
Is there some trouble brewing?   Do not hide it ;
Why keep us ignorant of coming ill?

Lady How. Child, you talk folly; what is there
    to hide?

Daughter. A long while since you bade the maids
    prepare
The great guest-chamber, but no guest has come.

Lady How. "Tis not to say that some guest may
    not come.

No, child, you're out, it is not that I fear.

Daughter. Northumberland and the Papists?

Lady How. Hush, be gone!

Run to the upper window, child, and say
If you see aught.

Daughter. What shall I look to see?

Lady How. Your father, child, who else? and let
me be.

[*Exit Child.*

Lady How. I sometimes think this life will drive
me mad.

Poor Lady Mary, it is worse for her;

But she must own that she has noble friends.

My husband does his part for her, that's certain.

Enter Lord Howard.

Lord How. Thought you, good wife, that I would
never come?

Lady How. I never thought to see you here again.

Lord How. Maybe thou'lt have more reason in
that thought

Ere all is over: 'tis a troublous time.

Lady How. I thought that all men favoured
Lady Mary.

Lord How. If she come here alive; but oh, that
    ride!
Men call me brave, but I would fear that ride,
When every tree or dyke or bush of thorn
May hide a traitor! 'Tis a fearful thought.
If she is taken we must fight for life.
You'll take the children, dame, and fly to Holland;
You'll need your bravery then. No trembling, wench.
    Lady How. May God defend me in the time of
    need;
Women are feeble creatures at the best.
    Lord How. Think of the Princess!
    Lady How.   May Heaven pity her,
And us and ours that follow in her train.
             Enter Daughter.
    Daughter. Mother, I see a horseman on the road
Spurring toward us; in the cloud of dust
I scarcely can discern what man he is,
But it seems royal livery.
    Lord How.   God forbid!
She's taken then; her man would ride in mask.
    Lady How. O husband, fly; they will not think
    of us.

Daughter. Who's taken, mother? What does
    father mean?
You always talk in riddles.

Lady How.   Child, be quiet!
Where is the rider?

Daughter.   He is close at hand.
Do you not hear his horse? Will some one meet
    him?

Lady How. Go, child, and quickly haste to bring
    me word—
His height, shape, colour, and the very man,
And if you have made note of him before.

Lord How. Farewell, good wife, they will not do
    you harm,—
Not at the present,—you must dry your eyes;
Think of the children and what I have bid you.
All may be well; our fears may be for naught,
But it looks ill.

Lady How.   Oh, speak not, stay not,
Husband dear, be gone.   I'll see him.

                 Enter Messenger.

Mess. Madam, I crave your pardon for my haste,
The Princess Mary will be here anon.

The King, our master, died about this time
Last even, and my royal mistress comes
In utmost haste to seek protection here.

 Lord How. (*bursting out from concealment*). Man,
  · the best words I ever lived to hear
Your lips have uttered! Ha! the Queen is safe,
The peace of England follows on that safety!
Ho, fellows, fetch the choicest vintage forth.
The Queen is safe. Long live the Queen of
  England!
Drink to her health, drink all to her salvation,
We'll have no stinting here.

 Mess. Her gracious Majesty is close at hand,
Spent with the weariness of her long ride.

 Lord How. Let all give welcome,—no, 'twere
  better not.
Wife, daughter, children, welcome home your Queen.
         [*Exeunt.*

Re-enter Princess Mary, with Lord Howard, Lady
Howard, and party.

 Lord How. Poor is this dwelling for a royal lady,
But loyal hearts will give you of their best.

 Princess. It is enough! I am o'ercome with joy

And weariness and gratitude to all.

You are too good, I have no words to speak,

Nor deeds to recompense your love to me.

 Lady How. Ah, madam! you are weary with

  your ride.

 Princess. Aching in every bone, but thank God

  safe !

And what can I in this extremity

But weep and pray, and pray and weep again

 Lord How. Hark to that shout, it is my armed

  retainers,

Who shout for joy that you are Queen of England.

 Princess. Last night it was a kingdom or a

  scaffold :

But for you, friend, before this very hour

My head had fallen upon the traitor's block.

But Heaven is merciful, and I am here,

And tears become not my deliverance.

 Lord How. Madam, here's wine, the choicest of

  our store.

 Princess. No wine like joy, I scarce yet know

  myself,

The weight of twenty years is rolled away ;

Oh, if deliverance can purchase good,
That good is all your own and ever must be!
But I am faint, my heavy eyelids close,
Pray you, I have not far to find my room.
I've much to speak of, but 'tis fruitless now,
To·morrow we shall talk on what hath chanced.

Act III.

Scene I.—The Tower.

Lord and Lady Northumberland.

Lord North. I've staked my all upon a desperate
throw !

Lady North. Good sir, be calm.

Lord North. Fill up the cups ! Damnation to the
hag !
She has no cause to love me.

Lady North.　　　　　　　Sir, no more.

Lord North. No pomp, nor power, nor circum-
stantial bravery,
Can ever pay for greatness.—Three days past
In all but name I was the king of England
And now—

Lady North. You will be more not less.

Lord North.　　　　　　　Who knows ?

The evils I have seen on other lives
Oppress my fancy: death with unsheathed sword
Stands betwixt me and her: the one goes down
And Heaven knows which.

Lady North. Banish these thoughts, ill augury
bodes success.

Lord North. Fortune's the merest fribble, no way
kind,

She loves to trick men with an alien splendour,
To lift the poor and set them among princes,
Only to dash them madly from their place
And teach them the uncertainty of pride.
Man's power is but a cable spun of sand,
A gossamer-web, a bodiless appearance,
A rainbow-tissued nothing—gilded ruin.

Lady North. Who yield to humour lend themselves
to loss:

Think of your points of vantage.

Lord North. Dearest wife !
Success comes sweeter when beyond our hope.

Lady North. You are again yourself: have the
lads come?

Lord North. Their delay bodes disaster.

D

Lady North.   Peace ! they come.
Let me go, husband.   Ambrose !

Enter Ambrose.

Lord North. No need to speak, she's fled.

Ambrose.   With all her household.

Lord North. Our luck, too.   Whither ?

Ambrose.   Sir, to Keninghall.
Or so we heard—for we could gather naught
More certain than her flight.

Lord North.   More mischief still.

Ambrose. The Lords in Council, sir, await you
    now.

Lord North. Damn them for traitors; not a man
    is true !
Have they heard aught?

Ambrose.   Not, sir, from me.

Lord North. Well, I must see them.   Say I'll
    see them here.
We'll face the truth, 'tis folly to conceal;
And flaws in fortune are retrieved by guile.

Enter the Lords in Council, with Lady Suffolk.

North. Shall we await the presence of the
    Queen ?

Lady Suffolk. She has retired to her own cham-
    ber, sir,
O'erwearied with the pressure of the time.
   Lord North. We will not vex her then. Your
    pardon, sirs,
That we have kept you. Tidings that are slow
Oft come most welcome. Lady Mary's gone.
Some say to Holland, leaving so the kingdom,
A weighty charge for one not born to rule,
Therein methinks proving her better wisdom.
   Pembroke. She is not here then.
   Lord North.   No, sir, she is not here :
Nor is it known for truth which way she fled ;
Some say she waits the issue of affairs
In Norfolk : 'tis a likely reasoning.
   Arundel. And you will fetch her thence ?
   Lord North.   'Twere wisest so.
   Pembroke. If she be there the east will surely
    rise.
   Lord North. They had fought anyway ; we looked
    for that.
   Lady Suffolk. O, sir, I pray you, do not do her
    ill ;

Why should a woman mix in state affairs?
She'll yield to fortune; trust a woman for't.

    Lord North. And if she did, her friends would
      still resist.

Two Queens can never share in sovereignty.

    Northampton. Will you to Norfolk then?

    Lord North.   Therefore I called you
To weigh the matter well before we act.
But prudence urges me to keep the city,
And guard the Sovereign in her novel state.

    Arundel. Suffolk can stay.

    Suffolk.   Your counsel, sir, is ready;
I may not wish to stay.

    Arundel.   O proper stuff!
You know you always do what others want.
Northumberland must go.

      Enter Messenger with letter from Queen
          Mary.

    Arundel to Pembroke. What missive makes the
      Lord Protector pale?

    Pembroke. Hush! he imparts the news!

    Lord North. My lords, this letter comes most
      opportune,

And shows the light where we were most perplexed.
The Princess is in Norfolk.

    Northampton.   Then you'll go.

    Lord North. I will not leave the city yet a while.
Suffolk, will you take guidance of my sons
In their rash youth? You, Warwick, go with them.
Pembroke, I'll keep you here, if't be your will.
But you, Northampton, would be well with them;
We must not clothe the field to strip the city,
But leave a power in both.

    Suffolk.   When shall we start?

    Lord North. To-morrow at your earliest: ere you
      rest
I would impart some counsel in affairs.
Can you attend me now, or must we wait?
I need not keep you further, gentlemen.
Ladies, adieu!

            [*Exeunt all but Lady Suffolk and Lady*
                Northumberland, Pembroke, and
                Arundel.

      Enter Guildford, Lady Jane following.

    Guildford. Gentlemen, mother, all, is this the truth—
I am not King of England?

Lady North.   Who denies?

Guildford. My wife, now in her chamber.   Here
    she comes,

To Arundel and Pembroke in hot haste.

        Enter Lady Jane.

Lady Jane. Tell me, my lords, what is it that I hear

Of Guildford's coronation?   Can it be

Without my knowledge Guildford is a King

Ere the assembling of my Parliament?

It fears me, sirs, ye do but mock my youth;

But think me not, though young, so ill advised

As not to know the limit of my powers;

And if ye counsel rash and hasty acts

In this, my lords, ye act not as my friends.

    Guildford. I am a King, proud girl, if you are
        Queen.

    Lady Jane. The crown to me came by direct
        command,

But Edward named no Guildford in his will.

And if I overstep my natural scope

And give a King to an unready people,

Then I, the very soul and fount of justice,

In my own person do pervert its sway.

Lady North. So wise a Queen can scarce need
　　help to rule!
She's wit enough to guide the universe.
Why should she seek the poor advice of men?

　　Lady Jane. Madam, it is my right to search the
　　truth,
Such words are ill-becoming.

　　Guildford.　　　　　　　　Haughty spouse!
No wife will ever bear the rule o'er me;
I will be King, proud girl, be sure of that,
If you are Queen. Think you I'll be your slave?
You greatly err.

　　Lady Jane. It is not, Guildford, want of love to you,
Nor over-greed for power that makes me speak;
But that you are a King is not the truth,—
And what is not the truth is all a lie,
And they do err who shut their eyes to light,
Walking blindfold in error.

　　Lady North.　　　　　　　Thankless chit!
Who takes the trouble that will make you Queen?

　　Lady Jane. My lords, have you no counsel in
　　distress?
Am I not right? I cannot but be right.

Arundel. There is no precedent for either case;
Your unwed cousins have been set aside
Lest by their marriage they might harm the State.
  Guildford. Then I am King!
  Lady Jane.   If so, who rules the land?
If power be equal, I am set aside
To whom the crown was due : what sense in that?
Why should the King leave me an empty honour?
  Guildford. Who argues with a woman?   They've
      no wit
To know when they are beaten.   I shall go.
So great a Queen can never own a husband ;
Go, boast yourself in solitary state
That you are Queen of England.   I am King.˙
                                        [*Exit.*

  Lady North. That is the way to reverence a
      husband !
You've taught us what those books mean.   Heaven
      be praised
I never pressed my girls with too much learning.
But I must after him and curb this humour,
Or else you'll rue the end o't.
                                        [*Exit.*

Lady Suffolk. Take no heed:
They're all alike, Jane; never speak the truth
If you would live in comfort. You're too open.

 Arundel. It is Northumberland supports your
  cause,
'Tis scarcely wise to thwart him; he is one
That can both make and mar you.

 Lady Jane. This is strange.
Am I the Queen, or does his father rule?

 Arundel. Initiate rule totters without support;
You must make peace with Guildford.

 Lady Jane. When he's wrong—
I cannot——

   Enter Warwick.

 Warwick. My lords, do ye prolong your confer-
  ence?
'Tis long past midnight; you detain the Queen
Beyond all reason. Shall I bid them go?

 Lady Jane. Will they not wait? the roads are
  dark at night,
And the mire heavy with the recent rain.

 Pembroke. The moon shines full and floods the
  way with brightness;

Much is to do before the break of day.
We'll leave you, madam, with your pardon now.
Think on my words at leisure.

[Exeunt.

  Lady Jane. Oh, mother, mother, everything is
    strange !
I'll play the Queen no more; they're fooling me.
When I came up the Watergate to-day,
All stared at me as I had been a show,
Or one that had gone mumming out of time.
I scarce know what to think on't.

  Lady Suff. You young folk think too much about
    yourselves !'
The year or two that gives you woman's grace
Bewilders those who class you as a babe.
My child, the Londoners scarce know your name;
Your welcome need not vex you.

  Lady Jane.   Very strange
The people should not know their future Queen.

  Lady Suff. The young King's death possesses all
    their thought.

  Lady Jane. 'Tis true: I had not thought o't.
    Dearest mother,

This bustling drives out every gentle thought.
No wonder men are hard; I cannot think,
Or feel, or do beyond the present instant.
Let us to rest.　You're weary, so am I.

SCENE II.—FRAMLINGHAM.

Queen Mary and Lady Ann Wharton.

Lady Ann. Madam, I pray you, rest.
Queen.　　　　　　　The mind's too full.
Mere bodily rest is naught.　I've much to write.
　Lady Ann. Let me write for you, madam, with
　　your words;
You want the use of bodily fatigue.
　Queen. Joy banishes fatigue.　Think, this day
　　week !
　Lady Ann. I tremble yet to think on't.
　Queen.　　　　　　　　　I rejoice:
Life's changefulness is like an opal gleam
On a dull tissue, thereby glorified;
The mystery of change gives point to joy

And sweetens pain, since who can tell the bliss
Hid behind life's next turning.   So with me.

   Lady Ann. Madam, indeed, 'tis cause of thank-
     fulness.

   Queen. My nature withered in obscurity,
For I was born to rule.   Labour itself
Wearies me less than dull vacuity.
Give me the letters.   Have you marked them yet?

   Lady Ann.   Here, madam.

   Queen. In all this joy are two great drops of
     bitter—

The stuff that tears are made of.   Silent and chill
The King lies in his chamber, far away
From civil discord and neglect of friends,
He rests in peace, poor boy! none cares for him,
So late the care of all.

   Lady Ann.   'Tis terrible!
No guard of honour, no repose of state;
The Lord Protector's mad to leave him thus,
So late the lord and master of us all.

   Queen. Death is his master now; the other grief
Is a more living gall: Lady Elizabeth,
Shut in her chamber with a feigning sickness, .

Writes not a word to me nor to the other
Until she sees who wins. I hate such craft;
But who gets grapes from thistles? She is deep—
Just like her mother; but she's won the people
With smooth hypocrisy and cunning ways.
I'll have my trouble with her, that I know,
She'd better have a care.

Enter Usher.

The Duke of Norfolk waits.

Norf. Madam, great news!
Northumberland proclaims you Queen in Cambridge.

Queen. Is't possible he can have stooped so low?
The appalling wickedness of men confounds me!
Had I so pledged myself as he has done,
I would have torn my tongue out by the roots
Sooner than bate one jot of her fair title
Whom I had named my Queen: her cause is lost.
Without a drop of bloodshed I am Queen.
Therefore the Lord be thanked.

Norf. Madam, the Lords are here,
Eager to swear allegiance.

Queen. Bid them approach:
I fear, sir, I may merit some reproach

By lack of recognition, for this morn
I saw their faces blurred as in a mist
Of mine expectancy. You must use skill
To abet my memory. Sussex is here and Bath,
I know some others, Wharton and Mordaunt, too,
The Jernynghams, besides I know some names,
But not the face to match them.

Enter various lords and gentlemen.

My Lord of Sussex, hail! Nay, sir, I shame
That one so reverend should bow the knee.
Prithee, sir, rise—unveil not,—the hoar head
Is as a crown, and Kings should not unveil
Before their fellows.

And Lord Wharton, too?
Dear for his own sake and his gentle sister.
My Lord of Bath! What a bold move was yours
To set me on the throne. You, too, and you—
So many more, no wonder I am Queen.
Oh, if devotion merit recompense,
Then I am yours in heart, and ever will be:
Ye shall forget the perils of the past
In tranquil peace; while righteousness and honour,
The noblest fruits of fair prosperity,

Shall grow for all beholders. Sirs, again,
I'll meet you all this evening, know my friends,
And pour the humble tribute of my thanks
On every faithful follower.

ACT IV.

SCENE I.—TOWER.

Lady Jane and her Waiting-Woman, Angela.

Lady Jane. Let me spin, Angela.
Angela.   Dear my lady,
The wheel's too heavy for the like of you.
Lady Jane. I'll try it anyhow, it makes a noise.
My mother will be here soon ; you can go.

> Shuttle, shuttle as you fly,
>   Tell me what my life is ?
> Young and simple maiden I,
>   But I know what strife is.
>   Turn treadle, run thread,
>   Joy and sorrow soon are sped.
>
> Shuttle, shuttle as you fly,
>   Tell me what is honour ?

She's a nymph so rare and shy,
  Few men look upon her.
    Turn treadle, run thread,
      Joy and sorrow soon are sped.

Shuttle, shuttle as you fly,
  Tell me what is duty?——

Enter Guildford.

Lady Jane. Guildford, what ails you? You are
  pale as death.

Guildford. Dead men are in this place. Come,
  let us go.

Lady Jane. These are strange words. Guildford,
  what do you mean?

Guildford. Who ever prospered yet that entered
  here?

I tell you 'tis a charnel house, a pit

Brimful of dead men's bones. It can tell secrets.

Lady Jane. Such horrid words betoken dreadful
  ill.

Speak, I entreat you.

    Guildford.   All are gone.

    Lady Jane.   Who?

E

Guildford. The Lords in Council; we are left
 alone.

Lady Jane. Whence heard you this?

Guildford.   I saw them all myself
Take boat upon the river.

Lady Jane.   They'll return.

Guildford. Yes, armed with city bands to take us
 prisoner.

Come, no delay, 'tis fatal. Let us leave—

While there is time, we will not have it long.

Lady Jane. Flight is the seal of guilt: I am not
 guilty,—

Not willingly at least; those were to blame

Who told me I was Queen. I cannot go

To escape the just recoil of wrongful deeds.

But you can go, you have no cause to stay.

Guildford. That's all you think of me: I have
 no honour,

I tell you, Jane, you never cared for me.

Lady Jane. What makes you speak so?

Guildford.   Hertford was a fool,—

And naught to look at either.

Lady Jane.   Why this Hertford?

Guildford. I am your husband, but you love me
  not.

Lady Jane. What have I done that you should
  speak like this?

Guildford. Done? Nothing: 'tis the root and
  ground of all,
You're just as kind to me as to most people,
And care as little. I would kiss the ground
Your feet have trod on.

Lady Jane.   When you left me, Guildford?

Guildford. I loved you all the same, I always
  loved you
From the first hour I saw you.

Lady Jane.   Men are strange:
Your will was never thought of in this marriage.
What would you have?

  Guildford. Scold me, Jane, roundly, and I'll know
  your love,
And I deserve it; but I'm naught to you,
Because I am no scholar.

Lady Jane.   Foolish boy!
The little more or less makes not much differ.
But I, in turn, will tell you you are out,

Thinking I care for Hertford more than you.

Why should I care for him or any man?

And yet it is my comfort that you love me,

For times are strange and everything is dark,

And you had left me, I was all alone.

Guildford, there's horses—go—why should you die?

　Guildford. I bide with you; it is not hard to
　die.

Enter Lady Suffolk.

　Lady Suff. Jane, Jane, what can this mean?
　What can it be?

Armed men are in the court—'tis full of them—

The city bands, and not a soul I know.

　Lady Jane. Mother, the Lords in Council are not
　here.

　Lady Suff. Impossible! they had a strait injunc-
　tion

To attend your presence here. What does it mean?

Enter Lord Suffolk, who tears down the canopy from
the royal seat.

　Lord Suff. Down with the canopy! You are no
　＼Queen,

My daughter, only an impostor here.

Lady Jane. But by King Edward's will I was
    made Queen,
And all the lords have sworn that this was true.
Are these oaths nothing?

Lord Suff.   Merest vanity :
They have gone over to your cousin's side.

Lady Jane. To me they swore allegiance and re-
    spect :
What is the meaning of this sudden change?

Lord Suff. Rats leave a sinking ship : your cause
    is lost,
And they have left.

Lady Jane.   . The Queen has faithful friends
If they serve her like me.   Then we can go,
And leave this horrid place like a bad dream.

Lord Suff. That may not be ; we all are prisoners
    here.
Expect the worst ; it may be we must die.

Lady Jane. Oh, what a web of evil ! Oh, my
    father !
Death and destruction follow in my wake.
O Guildford, heed me not—'tis life, 'tis life,
The surge of woe that beats about a throne.

I'll never blame you.   O my God, what blows
Must hammer souls to shape !

Enter Guards.

Guard. Gentlemen, you must go.   Your names
    are writ
Here in this paper, to be held apart.

Lady Suff. O husband, shall I never see you
    more?

Guildford. Your words are in my heart and in-
    finite sorrow
That I cause all this grief.

Lord Suff.   Farewell ! farewell !

Lady Jane. Oh, father !

Lord Suff.   Care for your mother, child ;
She needs it all.

           [*Exeunt Guards, with Lord Suffolk
           and Lord Guildford Dudley.*

Lady Jane. Oh, mother, mother, do not look like
    that.

Lady Suff. I knew this marriage never could bring
    good ;
When did alliance with deceitful men
Ever bring profit ?   Tush, my child, don't weep.

There's much to think of, and the others too—
If we are taken, Kate has got no sense.
Oh if my tears could wash away disaster
I'd melt my eyes, weeping for all this woe.
Tush, child, bear up.   We are together yet,
Why should you weep for him.   'Tis over now.

SCENE II.—WHITEHALL.

The Queen and Lady Ann Wharton.

Lady Ann. Madam, so young—
Queen.   Not so young, Lady Ann,
But he can be seditious.   You're too gentle:
Be firm and steel yourself against petition.
I wlll not hear requests.
Lady Ann.   · His mother, madam,
Spoke with such tears of his unguarded youth.
   Queen. Shall thousands groan in everlasting pain,
Because their leader was too feeble nerved
To lay the whip on foul and impious lies?
   Lady Ann. Truth is so various, madam, like a plant,

The root, leaves, stem, and blossom all diverse,
And he who hacks some dull unsightly root
May kill a living growth.

 Queen.   Ah, Lady Ann,
You are too simple-minded, think the best,
Trust each man's reasoning sooner than your own.
But truth is one, let not the present blind you;
We have had martyrs too, think on the past.
And they who prostitute the name of truth
T' include each specious form of private error
Would make of life a vast untrodden waste
Of incoherent purpose. Men are sick
Of wavering courses; there is no other way
To clear the rubbish from the path of truth.

  Lady Ann. Madam, I crave your pardon for bold
   speech.

  Queen. Oh, Lady Ann, thank Heaven upon your
   knees   .
You were not born to rule! Do right or wrong,
At every step I tread on bonded interests,
And disaffection like a serpent hides
Neath every courtly favour.
Look at this hand,—it is a little hand,

But it has signed death warrants. Woe the day !
Children must feel the rod, I must not flinch
From my stern duty, which is inch-meal death.
At the sword's point this anarchy must end ;
And I must fight alone with all these hounds
Barking at once; do violence to nature
At every hour and moment of the day—
That is to be a queen.

 Lady Ann.   But power is service
And present troubles soon will be at rest.

 Queen. But they come on, come on, like ocean's
  waves,
Each moment brings its little drop of bitter.

 Lady Ann. The strength is given to bear it.

 Queen.   No, it is not.
'Tis misery, misery, unending pain.

    Enter Usher.

The Austrian Ambassador waits.

    Enter Renard.

 Queen. Be near if I should call you.

      [*Exit Lady Ann.*

 Queen. Be seated, sir, have you had further counsel ?

 Renard. Are the lords still averse ?

Queen. I will not hear of Courtenay, that is fixed;
A churl not fit to match my serving maid,
But still they urge this marriage.

    Renard. What Englishman can match your royal
      state?

    Queen. None that I know, but they will have me
      wed.

    Renard. I know a match that might command
      the world.

    Queen. Ambition tempts me not, but dignity.

    Renard. Prince Philip matches you in royal state.

    Queen. These English lords detest all foreigners.

    Renard. But to your wish, at least, the lords must
      bow.

    Queen. Nay, self-advancement is in all their
      thought,
Scarce one in office but has sworn before
Allegiance to Northumberland's Queen Jane.

    Renard. That was a treacherous time. I scarce
      had hoped
To see you win your way so prosperously.

    Queen. I had the right, and London citizens
Pushed for me strongly. 'Twas a perilous time;

Yet, let me tell you, there were consolations
Exist no longer for the crownèd Queen.
I am a prisoner in my palace here,
Fenced round with jealous eyes at every turn,
And she, my hapless rival for the throne,
Enjoys more real liberty than I.

 Renard. This marriage would give strength.

 Queen.   A perilous cure.
Why should I raise a storm about my head
With vain proposals? I shall never wed.

 Renard. Not till the fitting princely partner comes.
Your Majesty is right: but were there one,
Young, rich and noble, equal in estate
To your own dignity, who came to sue,
Your maiden purpose would not say him nay.

 Queen. There's no such suitor, so my purpose
  stands.

 Renard. But there is one. I have his picture
  here.
Would't please you to regard it, not as one
Who sues unwelcome, but a gracious presence
Which there portrays itself in every line.

 Queen. Such a gay gallant would not suit with me.

I am old, Renard, and older in my heart
Than in my showing. I have suffered much.

Renard. Let future bliss obliterate past ill.

Queen. Oh, tempt me not with joy, I'll none of it,
For mirth was banished from my earliest years,
And bitter cups are those most fit for me.

Renard. Madam, it is the mind that makes the
man,
Not the mere count of swiftly passing years;
A younger woman has not got the scope,
The breadth of sympathy, the weight of counsel,
Which wakens love in such an august mind.

Queen. Oh, tempt me not from wisdom—let me
be.
I'll see you on the morrow, if you will.
Yet, stay, I'll keep the picture.

[*Exit Renard.*

Queen. I thought life had dealt niggardly with me,
But Heaven has sent me this. O most fair face !
I am the Queen of England : I have much,
And I will give you all. Oh ! I will love you,
Till you forget my years. Sweet sun of joy,
Risen on the darkness of my dreary days ! .

Enter Lady Ann.

Queen. Look, Lady Ann, is't not a noble face?

Lady Ann. Whose is the picture, madam?

Queen.   Oh, you are dull.
Think with what fools and dotards I am evened.

Lady Ann. I do not know the face.

Queen.   But you will know it.
Guess, and guess quickly : if you had a lover
Would you not choose that face?

Lady Ann.   Why, madam, no.
I'd choose the deed, not face.

Queen.   Oh, you are old,
And I begin my life : it is my suitor,
Philip, the Prince of Spain.   What think you now?

Lady Ann. Madam, Heaven make him worthy
            of your love,
For mortal born can never wholly meet
A woman's expectation.   May the fair face
Prove the fair pledge of nobleness unlimned !

Scene III.—Whitehall Council Chamber.

Deputation of Commons.

First Com. Another burnt at Lewes !

Second Com.   Monstrous ! What next ?

Third Com. Heaven only knows : the people will
   not stand it ;

They'll rise in arms and drive her from the throne.

First Com. We had been better with Northumberland ;

At any rate he saw our present case

With an unwedded woman on the throne.

No peace since she began, but endless trouble.

Fourth Com. He had slain hundreds where she
   slays her ten ;

. Men are like tigers when they once taste blood ;

And she began with scruples, he had none.

First Com. This marriage will but make the
   trouble worse ;

I wonder at a woman of her years

Doting upon a boy beyond all nature.

Second Com. He's not so young, sir, as his
    picture looks.
But love's like measles, worse when taken late.
    Third Com. They say he is as cruel as the grave.
They're matched in nature truly.
    Fourth Com. It is the people's fault from end to
    end ;
They did not know their mind, and she has taught
    them.
    Second Com. And she has taught them other than
    she thought !
I never grudged her saying of the mass,
Her altars, vestments, censers, and such like.
Somerset's whitewash was not to my mind,
But when it comes to burning folk alive
There's something wrong, I warrant.
    Fourth Com.   Think of the past—
The rank disorder and indecency.
Who did not cry for order?
    First Com.   Want of judgment
Breeds tenfold chaos, and the Queen has none.
    Fifth Com.   There's something more :
Is she to set the limits of Heaven's mercy,

And bound the Heavenly kingdom by her will?
Or who is judge?

 First Com. Hush! she comes.

   Enter the Queen and train.

Queen. Most honourable sirs, ye come right welcome,
To make request touching the common weal
And mine own welfare, wherefore speak your plea
And I shall hearken, as my bounden duty.

Speaker. To our most noble and religious Queen
The Lords and Commons of the realm send greeting:
For that your royal Grace should know their will,
Both for your health and for the general weal,
We here are present: we would thereto add
The great desire they have toward your marriage.
Wherefore, we humbly pray your royal Grace
Should marry soon with one of your own subjects.
A foreign prince might cumber much the state
With barbarous customs; further, he might use
The English wealth to our own detriment,
And, having English forces in control,
Might controvert them unto our own hurt;
Yea, he might bear your Highness from the land,
And rear your children in unwholesome ways.

Therefore your people humbly make request
That foreign suits be wholly set aside
As not conformable to native honour.

    Queen. Most honourable sirs, your zeal is great,
But in that ye would choose our royal spouse,
Your zeal, methinks, outsteps all decency.
It hath not been the wont of Parliament
Aforetime to direct its Sovereigns
What spouse to choose, nor is it fitting now.
Where private persons follow their own choice,
A Queen may surely have like liberty.
Much ye have said of marriage, but not much
Of what imports us—private inclination.
I have lived maiden all my years of life,
And maiden I will die if Heaven so please;
But, if my people force on me a spouse
Against my will, the evils that they dread
Will soon be on them, I'll not live to face't.
Our coronation oath is not forgot,
But I will marry me as God directs,
Unto His honour and the country's weal,
And follow no man's bidding. Are you answered?
Remove the Speaker.

                  F

Speaker is removed.

Queen. You, Gardiner, I thank for this affair.

Gardiner. I knew not their request, most royal
    lady,

They made their own petition and not I.

Queen. You should have᾿ seen that I was not
    insulted.

But this I know, you favour Courtenay's suit.

Gardiner. He was my fellow prisoner.

Queen.   'Tis fair reason

Why I, that am a Queen, should wed with him,

A foolish, ignorant, conceited ass.

I'll hear no more petitions for a time.

Gardiner. Did you not think to speak of the
    succession ?

Queen. The Commons have insulted me to-day,

Insulted me past bearing—I'll not stay :

When I am ready, I can summon them.

                              [*Exit.*

First Com. Of one commodity the Queen hath
    store,

To wit her temper; were it turned to coin

Her Grace's debtors would be quickly paid.

.

Act V.

Scene I.—Whitehall. Antechamber.

Cicely, a Waiting Gentlewoman.

Cicely. One, two.—That's ten and not out yet—
How can she love the Queen?—but some are saints.
        Enter Lady Ann.
You have been up all night—the Queen is cruel.
  Lady Ann. Hush, Cicely! hush. Her grace could
    get no sleep.
  Cicely. And so, forsooth, must keep her hand in
    yours
The whole night through; mere selfishness, I say.
  Lady Ann. The young are hard. It is my trivial
    service,
I was her friend ere ever you were born.
  Cicely. More reason she should spare you, heart-
    less thing.

Lady Ann. Cicely, what words! you know not
    what you say—
And but your heart is kinder than your speech,
I'd send you from me.
    Cicely.   Dearest Lady Ann!
She ought to yield; nobody wants the match;
Pure misery to herself and every one.
    Lady Ann. The young are ever wiser than the old;
You must be patient.
    Cicely.   Father Feckenham's here.
    Lady Ann. I want to see him ere he see the Queen.
    Cicely. I'll tell him then, he is a dear old soul.
    Queen (within). Blot out that name! I will not
    know it more—
My people, O my people, will you slay me?
    Lady Ann. Poor soul! poor soul!
           Enter Father Feckenham.
               Oh, sir, why are you here?
    Fecken. I thought yon summoned me.
    Lady Ann.   Not here, not here.
The Queen will soon be stirring. 'Tis her chamber.
    Fecken. How has her Highness slept?
    Lady Ann.   Sir, do not ask.

A dreadful night, the terrors of the past,
The toils and dangers of the last few months
All lived again in agony and in peril.

   Fecken. The marriage, too, is off.

   Lady Ann.   Believe it not.

   Queen (within). O Philip, Philip, Philip, but I love
       you !

My people, oh my people, slay me first !

   Lady Ann. All the night long for weeks she speaks
       like that,

Gazes upon his picture by the hour,
And all night long a lamp is lit beside it.
I crave your counsel, sir, in sore distress;
Such love is madness ; break her of this passion
By any means, or flesh and blood must fail.

   Fecken. What would you have me do ?

   Lady Ann.   Make her decide.

This wavering leads to madness.
None else has power or weight in speaking truth.
Surely in piety there must be help,
To you she may unburden. Hush ! she stirs.
Follow me hence, she must not see you here.

                            [*Exeunt.*

Enter the Queen.

Queen. How cold it is! I shiver with the cold,
These spring days wear a dagger in their brightness
That chills the blood like a deceitful friend.
Where's Lady Ann? Poor soul, perchance grown tired
Of waiting on me, I'll not press her service.

Enter Lady Ann.

If Father Feckenham's here, I'll see him now.

[*Exit Lady Ann.*

Queen. Oh for some charm to numb the power of
    thought!
Who left the glass there? Cicely, most like.
Her vanity wants reproof. Vile glass, you lie.
I am not yet so old, so hollow-eyed!
Oh, I am shattered, shattered, a mere wreck
Of what I was but a few months ago.
I would not ride that hundred miles again,
Not if my life were on't. 'Tis vanity.
I think that I could count my reign by years
Not months, the months have been so slow,
And all the hope, the life, the energy
Have been drained out of me.

                        Well, she must die;

There is no other way, she lived too long.
Oh, if my enemies were but this paper
How I would tear them into pieces, so !
But the worst evil is within this breast.

Enter Feckenham.

Good Father Feckenham, you see me changed ;
Am I much altered, tell me, in your eyes ?

Fecken. Your Majesty is weary, is it not ?
The last few days have worn out strength and spirit,
You have not yet recovered from the shock.

Queen. I am one quivering nerve of agitation,
Strung to vibration by suspense and pain.
Oh, it was fearful—every drop of blood
Stood still in terror—pity, pity me.
I stood alone, upon the portico—
No man was with me—all the seething mass
Yelling beneath me, mad with rage and drink,—
I chid the tremblers, roused the valiant-minded,
And won the day in face of desperation.

Fecken. A most courageous Queen.

Queen.   Mere self-defence.
If I had gone, my enemies would have won,
Perchance they might have torn me limb from limb.

There is no mercy in a furious mob,
And I have no affection from this people.

Fecken. You wrong yourself in over vehemence.
This people made you Queen.

Queen. I had forgot.
I hate them all, and every day I live
I seem to hate them more. Would I had died
Ere ever I was Queen. 'Tis but a mood,
I'll be myself anon. Saw you the Lady Jane?

Fecken. Madam, without avail.
She is so fixed and grounded in her faith
I have not yet dislodged her.

Queen. Latin and Greek
Were her undoing: she was ill brought up,
Spending her time on vain deceitful learning,
Scorning the holy teaching of the Church.

Fecken. She seems a child, and yet in innocence
Hath such a subtle power of weighty speech
I could not speak her home.

Queen. All of a piece.
She's obstinate, believe me, very stiff.
She spoilt her own promotion, made my heir
But for perversity. 'Tis over now.

Heard you how my Lord Suffolk was ta'en prisoner
Hid like a cat within a hollow tree.
But for his plots and her apostasy
She would have been the heiress to the throne.
Saw you the husband, Guildford Dudley, too?
 Fecken. He seems a very gentle, pleasant lad.
 Queen. The Dudleys are all handsome, more's
  the mischief.
Come, tell me more, you told them they must die?
 Fecken. And my heart bled to do't; it seemed
  more like
They were two self-willed lovers, and I paused,
Half doubting if the message could be true.
 Queen. Peace, Feckenham, peace, why do you
  stab me too?
It is my odious duty. Not my will.
 Fecken. He spoke most manly, bid me say adieu,
And tell his mistress he loved her alone,
And died twice over as her cause of death.
 Queen. Oh, she is happy! some one cares for
  her!
More than is true of me, the Queen of England.
Who would shed tears for me if I were gone,

An uneasy riddle that men cannot solve?
Oh, father, all my heart is but one wound,
And whom I love most, writes me not one word
In all this trouble which himself has caused.
It is the crown he weds and not the woman.
Why should he seek a wan, ill-favoured bride,—
And how I crave his love,—hunger and thirst,
Die for affection,—only Heaven can know.

Fecken. My daughter, love is but the hungry heart
Preying upon its own imagination;
There is no food, nor can there ever be
In phantom banquets on earth's wilderness.
I, who am old, have oft time pondered this,
Why life and joy and energy and strength
Are spent on vain delusions.

Queen.   Oh, not vain!
Surely on this side time there is some truth,
Life were a mockery else and love is peace.

Fecken. My daughter, half the ills that cumber
          earth
Spring from no other source.

Queen.   It is not true,
It is the mastery over life in time.

Fecken. The world was conquered in reproach and
  shame
And in self mastery of wilful thought.

Queen. But I have nothing else.

Fecken.   You have your people,
Turn your eyes round you and your heart will fill.

Queen. I was not born to rule, I hate this people,
No gratitude, no mercy, endless grumbling.
Pray for me, holy father,
The most unhappy woman in the land.
Pray that in victory, I may have peace.
I cannot, no, I will not give him up
Who is the spouse ordained for me by Heaven,
The champion and defender of the faith.
Yet Philip, though I love him—oh, is cruel,
Cruel to me who love him—I am mad—
Brain weary, father, sick at the heart,
Therefore I utter words bereft of meaning.
Leave me, sir, I must rest.

Fecken. Shall I call some one, madam, to your aid?

Queen. No, leave me thus, I shall do well alone;
Men mark my face, and set it in their books,
And peer on me with idle, curious eyes.

So I must smile and counterfeit glad cheer
While the heart gnaws within. I'll rest and rest
And gather up my powers for that great strife.
I know I was not throned for my own good,
The misery of my soul can teach me that;
But to be champion of the Holy Church,
To fight its battles, and defend its cause,
And stem the encroaching tide of heresy,
That is a task beyond a giant's strength,—
That I, mere woman, should be chosen out
To compass this great end is recompense,
Greater reward than any earthly bliss.

.

Scene II.—The Tower.

Lady Jane and her Waiting-Woman, Angela.

Lady Jane. When say you they will pass?
Angela.   Their warden said
To-day about this hour or somewhat later.
Lady Jane. And I shall see him and my father too.
Ah! Angela, I want so much to see them.
The Queen sent word that I might see my husband,
And I refused, the parting seemed so brief,

Scarce worth the weeping for—but I was wrong—
Not that I wanted love but I lacked wisdom.
Oh ! Angela, death is so hard for him—
So young, so strong, so full of life and vigour.
I might have smoothed the sullen way of death
And made it easier, but I thought my thoughts
Unmindful of his wish. I would not see him.
Yet, Angela, he loved me all the time,
Loved me, poor me, without a charm to win him,
When he was handsome beyond other men.

>   *Angela.* 'Twas but a slight return for all this
>   trouble.

>   *Lady Jane.* No, no, not slight, far more than my
>   desert,

He taught me more than all the books I read;
Life is a nobler school for thought than words
And far more hard to master.

>   Angela !

I'm dying now, you will not grudge my speech
For all the years I've wasted : this I think,
Men miss life's teaching in ´untutored thought.
Now in a crabbed passage of the Greek
I'd pause, weigh words, each letter, point and phrase,

Nor think my private judgment was the right
Without due reasoning; but on a soul
I'll pass my judgment with less pause to think
Than put my thought in words. Now life is past
And every jot of teaching thrown away
Upon an ignorant scholar. That's my life.
O learn the lesson of a wasted life and reverence
    all men.

Hush! do you hear? that's horses. They are come.
I'll put my whole soul in one smile to him,
And smile to him as I should wish he'd smile
To welcome me in heaven.

   Angela. Back from the window! dear my lady,
    back !

Oh I implore you, I entreat you stay !

   Lady Jane. You must not keep me back from my
    own husband.

   (*Lady Jane sees the lifeless bodies of husband and
    father carried from the place of execution.*)

                 [*She faints.*

   Angela. O Heaven, prove merciful, let this be death.
Alas, dear child, your death should cause me joy ;
But no—she wakes to taste the bitter end.

Lady Jane. Angela, have they passed ?—I had
    forgot—
All marred by villains, cruel, cruel sight.
Angela, I try to think of heavenly things
But the tears blind me. Oh ! good Angela,
I·pray you do not come with me to-day.
Sir John will see that every thing is right,
And all men know I was a modest woman—
A Princess too—and will not see me wronged.
Indeed, good Angela, I do not want you ;
For if I did, then I would bid you come.
    Angela.   O most dear lady,
Your head has lain upon this bosom once ;
Little thought I that my sweet lady's head
Wonld ever lie upon a bloody pillow.
Oh, I had sooner thought to see you crowned
With all the pomp and state by the King's side,
And this the end !—
Shame on the black heart of Northumberland !
Shame on the bloody Queen that this should be !
Shame and thrice shame upon the laws of England
That let the guiltless suffer for the guilty.
O my sweet lady, I have seen you Queen,

Followed you through each changing chance of life,
And, think you, I could ever leave you, sweet,
And let you go to face your death alone?
No, my dear lady, that can never be.
Were death the penalty, I'd sooner die..

    Lady Jane. You have been good to me my whole
      life long.

But all have been more kind than I deserved.
Though life was short, I have had many friends.
It comforts me in sorrow. Even the Queen
Would save me in this pass if she had power,
But dares not risk her people's peace for me.
I think I understand it, Angela—
I was a Queen, though for so short a time,
I felt the pulse of a whole nation's life
Throb through my veins,—I seem to feel it still,—
I think I should have felt it till I died.
And Queens are different from humbler folk,—
The hearts of kings are in God's governance,—
And that is true when every slip and error
Seems an unfathomable gulf of woe,
And men's blood flows for some unhappy flaw
Would pass unnoticed in a lesser woman.

I oft times think how much I have been spared.
The Queen has had to suffer all alone.

Angela. She is a wicked murderess, no less!

Lady Jane. Power is an awful thing in troublous
    times :

Think upon this with pity.

Angela. I will not pity her—I never can.

Lady Jane. Our Lord had mercy on His tor-
    turers ;

They knew not what they did, nor does the Queen.
There's some things, Angela, that I would tell you ;
I wrote them in this paper for my mother.
Here are my rings—I shall not want them more.
This with the portrait to young Robert Dudley;
My grandmother it is—men say like me.
I think that's all. Though I was Queen of Eng-
    land

I have not much that I can call my own.

Angela. O my dear lady, do not break my heart;
Who cares for anything when you are gone?

Lady Jane. Not now, perhaps, but time heals
    every ill.

I'd not have any slighted. I must go.

G

This is the saddest and the gladdest day
Of all my life: my childhood was a dream:
And that strange spell of trembling exaltation
Is only like a dream within a dream.
My mind is dazed with my approaching joy,
And all the sorrow, all the mystery
Dazzles my eyes like sunlight seen through tears
I must apart to commune with myself
Till the great moment.

[*Exit.*

Angela. Who knocks without?

Feckenham. Open—'tis I.

Enter Father Feckenham.

Fecken. How! she is gone! I had not thought
so soon.

Angela. My lady has retired herself to pray.

Fecken. I must have speech with her before she
go.

Angela. Oh, sir, I pray you do not vex her now.

Fecken. Woman, I must speak with her ere she
go.

Angela. Oh, it is cruel to torment her thus,
And stint the precious moments of her prayer.

Fecken. Woman, I tell you I must speak with her.
Compassion cannot make me fail in duty.

Angela. Then wait without, sir, till I hear her will.
Madam, the priest who talked with you before
Is urgent here to see you.

Lady Jane. Has the Queen sent him?

Angela. Yes, she has bid him come.

Lady Jane. Bring him within.
My heart is so fulfilled with thankfulness,
I am so rooted and built up in joy,
His words can scarce distress me.

Enter Feckenham.

Fecken. Dear lady, have you pondered, have you
    thought,
Have you weighed well my words of yesterday?
O wandering lamb, why will you leave the fold?
Turn from the error of your perverse ways,
And cast presumptuous heresy aside.

Lady Jane. Nay, by the Truth I hold, the Living
    Way,
And therein trust I shall not wholly err,
Knowing whose merits purged my guilty soul,
And mine iniquity washed clean away.

Fecken. In confidence you err, and vain con-
ceit,—

Who but the Bride can grace the marriage feast?

The spotless Bride, the heart's supreme desire,

The Holy Church, one, indivisible,

The noble company of faithful souls,

Whose fellowship you fondly cast aside.

Turn at the eleventh hour—there still is room—

The Church can still receive you to her breast;

Why will you cast your virtue's crown aside

For endless ruin, everlasting woe.

Lady Jane. Speak not to me with vain, presumptuous words !

A righteous Judge will judge your soul and mine;

Man's judgment pains me not — I know my
ground. ·

I think in heaven will be some little place

Where I may pray and praise for evermore. ·

Fecken. Oh, child ! you err—you know not how
you err ;

You break my heart with weeping.

Lady Jane. Father, the time is past for idle
words,

The dial points the hour that I must die,
And I must hasten to prepare for death.

Fecken. Farewell, my child, we shall not meet
again.

Lady Jane. Nay, we shall never meet except you
change.

But you have life, and truth is very wide;
The gates of heaven are open every day.
I thank you, sir, for your great courtesy,
Albeit I cannot, no, nor ever could
Accept your guidance; you have utterance
Which may Heaven turn to better purposes.

[*Exit.*

Angela. Who knocks without?

Mistress Underhill. Open to me, 'I pray;
I have allowance—Mistress Underhill.

Angela. Ye will not be so greedy of her time
To stint the precious moments of her prayer.
If ye have mercy, spare my mistress now.

Lady Jane. Angela, who waits upon me at this
hour?

Angela. 'Tis Mistress Underhill with her young
babe.

Lady Jane. Let her be welcome : brief the space
    of time
For kindly words, but all eternity
For praising God.

Mistress Underhill. This is your god-son, madam,
I brought him for a blessing ere you went.

Lady Jane. I can remember—that brief spell of
    time
When I was called in mockery Queen of England.
I thought to do the babe some favour then
When he was older, but that all is past.
Look how he smiles upon his god-mother.
Alas ! poor babe, she cannot help thee now.
May he live long and be a comfort to you,
All other joys go with a parent's blessing.
Yet were his life as mine 'twere not amiss,
For after brief affliction I have joy.
A step is on the stairs ; good mistress, go.

    Enter Sir John Gates, with soldiers.

Sir J. Gates. Most noble, come.   Would I were
    in your place.

Lady Jane. Sir, it will soon be over.   Angela,
    farewell.

Tell my dear mother that I feared not death.
Father, farewell.   What, you will come with me?
Farewell, gentlemen, I'll not speak more.   Farewell.

THE END.

www.ingramcontent.com/pod-product-compliance
Lightning Source LLC
Chambersburg PA
CBHW022342020726
47500CB00004B/1245